Animal
Alphabet
Christmas

By: Emmett Sutherland

For my family and friends

The animals all gathered around the tree to open Christmas presents.

Aiden the ape was given an apron for Christmas.

Aiden the ape is a chimpanzee. A chimpanzee is an endangered species that lives in Africa. Chimpanzees know how to make and use tools to help them live.

Benny the black bear was given a book for Christmas.

Benny is a black bear. Black bears live in North America. They live in forests and are very good at climbing trees.

B b

Carl the capybara was given a clock for Christmas.

Carl is a capybara. Capybaras are giant long-legged rodents who live in South America. They have webbed feet and are excellent swimmers.

Cc

David the dog was given a doll for Christmas.

David the dog is a dalmatian. A dalmation is a medium-sized spotted dog. Dalmations used to protect horses from wild animals when they pulled coaches; now they like fire engines.

Dd

Ezekiel the eel was given an electric blanket for Christmas.

Ezekiel is a moray eel. Moray eels live in oceans all over the world and they like warm water. They hide in coral reefs and rocks and hunt fish to eat.

Ee

Freddie the fossa was given a fan for Christmas.

Freddie is a fossa. Fossas are mammals that live in the forests of Madagascar. They have sharp teeth and claws and eat meat, mainly feeding on lemurs.

Ff

Gary the gerenuk was given glue for Christmas.

Gary is a gerenuk. Gerenuks are long-necked, long-legged antelopes that live in Africa. They can stand on their rear legs to reach leaves and buds on trees and they can survive a long time without water.

Harvey the hippopotamus was given a hat for Christmas.

Harvey is a hippopotamus. Hippopotamuses are large mammals that live in Africa. They love to be in the water and their name means "water horse".

Hh

Ivy the ibis was given an iron for Christmas.

Ivy is a scarlet ibis. Scarlet ibises live in tropical South America and on islands of the Caribbean. They get their red color from eating a lot of red food, like shrimp and crayfish.

James the jerboa was given a jack-in-the-box for Christmas

James is a jerboa. Jerboas are hopping rodents that live in the deserts of Arabia, northern Africa, and across Asia. Jerboas don't drink water, they get all their moisture from the food they eat, like plants and insects.

Jj

Kimi the kangaroo was given a kite for Christmas.

Kimi is a kangaroo. Kangaroos are large, hopping marsupials who live in Australia and Tasmania. Kangaroo babies are called "joeys". They are born very tiny and can live in their mother's pouch for almost a year.

Kk

Larry the lammergeier was given a lion for Christmas.

Larry is a lammergeier. Lammergeiers are also known as bearded vultures and they live in Europe, Africa, and Asia. They are scavengers and mostly eat bones, which they crack open on large rocks by flying overhead and dropping them.

LI

Martin the manatee was given a mask for Christmas.

Martin is a manatee. Manatees are large mammals that live in the waters of the Caribbean Sea, Gulf of Mexico, West Africa, and the Amazon Basin. They are slow-moving and gentle herbivores and are sometimes called "sea cows".

Mm

Ned the numbat was given a notebook for Christmas.

Ned is a numbat. Numbats are also known as banded anteaters and live in Australia. They are insectivores and eat a lot of termites and other insects.

Nn

Owen the okapi was given an oboe for Christmas.

Owen is an okapi. Okapis are hoofed mammals that live in the forests of Central Africa. They are related to giraffes. The tongues of okapis are so long, they can wash their eyelids and clean their ears.

Oo

Percy the pangolin was given pants for Christmas.

Percy is a pangolin. A pangolin is a scaly anteater that lives in Africa and Asia. They are burrowing mammals that eat ants and termites. They are very shy and when they get scared they curl into a ball.

Pp

Quincy the quail was given a quilt for Christmas.

Quincy is a California Quail. California Quails are ground-dwelling birds that live in the western United States. They are the state bird of California. Quails like to find soft patches of soil and take baths in the dust.

Qq

Ryan the rhinoceros was given a radio for Christmas.

Ryan is a black rhinoceros. Black rhinos are large mammals that live in Africa. They are very endangered and are at risk of becoming extinct. Their horns are made of keratin, just like human finernails and toenails.

Rr

Sidney the saiga was given some socks for Christmas.

Sidney is a saiga. Saigas are antelopes with a small, shortened trunk and can be found in flat grasslands in Mongolia. They are very endangered and at risk of becoming extinct. People hunt saigas for their horns.

Ss

Timothy the tiger was given a teddy bear for Christmas.

Timothy is a Bengal tiger. Bengal tigers are very large cats that live in the forests of India. They are endangered and at risk of becoming extinct. A tiger's roar can be heard as far as two miles away.

Tt

Ulysses the Utahraptor was given a unicycle for Christmas.

Ulysses is a Utahraptor. Utahraptors are an extinct dinosaur that lived in North America over 125 million years ago. At 25 feet long from head to tail, it is by far the biggest raptor that ever walked the earth.

Uu

Vinnie the vicuna was given a vest for Christmas.

Vinnie is a vicuna. Vicunas are hoofed mammals that live high in the Andes Mountains of South America. They are related to llamas and alpacas and people use their wool to make clothing.

Vv

Wilbur the whale was given a wagon for Christmas.

Wilbur is a blue whale. Blue whales are large marine mammals that live in the North Atlantic and North Pacific oceans. They are the largest living creature to have ever lived on earth. Blue whales can eat as much as four tons of tiny shrimplike animals called krill a day.

Re**x** the o**x** was given a fo**x** for Christmas.

Rex is an ox. Oxen are large-horned mammals that once moved in wild herds across many of the world's continents. They have been domesticated by humans for over 6,000 years, working in fields, pulling wagons, and for other agricultural purposes.

Xx

Yogi the yak was given a yo-yo for Christmas.

Yogi is a yak. Yaks are large domesticated wild oxen from Asia with shaggy hair, humped shoulders, and large horns. They are used as a pack animal and for its milk, meat, and hide.

Zeke the zebra was given a Zumbaa* for Christmas.

* a Zumbaa is a plush alien animal from Saturn.

Zeke is a zebra. Zebras are horse-like mammals that live in the grasslands of Africa. They have black and white stripes that are different for each one.

Zz